THE
MAGIC MENORAH
A Modern Chanukah Tale

<small>BY</small> Jane Breskin Zalben
<small>ILLUSTRATED BY</small> Donna Diamond

Simon & Schuster Books for Young Readers
New York • London • Toronto • Sydney • Singapore

Simon & Schuster Books for Young Readers

An imprint of Simon & Schuster Children's Publishing Division

1230 Avenue of the Americas, New York, New York 10020

Book design by Paul Zakris

The text for this book is set in 16-point Granjon.

The illustrations are rendered in graphite.

Printed in the United States of America

2 4 6 8 10 9 7 5 3 1

Library of Congress Cataloging-in-Publication Data

Zalben, Jane Breskin.

The magic menorah : a modern Chanukah tale / by Jane Breskin Zalben ; illustrated by Donna Diamond— 1st ed.

p. cm.

Summary: Stanley does not look forward to spending another Chanukah with all his relatives, but when an old man comes out of a tarnished menorah in the attic and grants Stanley three wishes, he changes his mind.

ISBN 0-689-82606-0

[1. Hanukkah—Fiction. 2. Family life—Fiction. 3. Jews—Fiction.] I. Diamond, Donna, ill. II. Title.

PZ7.Z254 Mag 2001

[Fic]—dc21   00-045058

FIRST
EDITION

For Steven Zalben—my inspiration on this page and off—
who thought of the story, and to Papa "Fishel,"
wherever you are—J. B. Z.

To Bob, with love—D. D.

Contents

"A lamp is a mitzvah
and the Torah is the light."

—PROVERB FOR CHANUKAH (PROVERBS 6:23)

CHAPTER ONE

The Box in the Attic

Once upon a time, in a small village not too far from a large shopping mall, there lived a boy named Stanley Green. He had everything in the world a child could ever want or need. And so, since the first night of Chanukah was beginning at sunset that evening, Stanley's parents wondered what more they could possibly give him.

As usual, Stanley's relatives were

coming. The house always got hot, noisy, and stuffy. Great-Aunt Sophie would give mushy, wet kisses and would pinch his cheeks. Uncle Max would squash him in a bear hug and breathe hot onion breath on his face. When his younger cousins Nathan, Ernie, and Emma came over, they always fought and yelled, and made a mess of all his things. That meant a lot of picking up and cleaning up after them. And Grandpa Abe, who always told the best stories the rest of the year, became quiet and sad during Chanukah. Stanley just wasn't looking forward to the holiday season.

Stanley's mother, Mrs. Green, hummed to herself as she covered the dining-room table with Grandma's lace tablecloth and linen napkins. Then she began to prepare for the Chanukah meal.

The kitchen buzzed with the sound of mixing and grating. Stanley peeled potato after potato. He grated so many potatoes that his knuckles were almost as raw as the potatoes he had peeled. His mother paused from chopping onions. She opened the kitchen window a bit and breathed in the cool night air. "Ah, those onions are sharp," she said, wiping her eyes as she added the onions to the latke batter. It was heaped high as a mountain in a ceramic bowl. "My tears could fill this bowl," she laughed.

As Stanley peeled and grated more potatoes, and applesauce bubbled in a big pot on the stove, his mother suddenly hit her forehead with the back of her hand. "Oh, no! I forgot to buy cinnamon for the applesauce! Stanley, I need you to help out while I run to the corner store." She continued as she put on her coat and gloves. "You know the large trunk in the attic? Inside is an old box covered with lots of foreign stamps. Grandpa Abe asked us to get it out for him this Chanukah. It would be a great help to me if you would do that. The box is from your Great-Uncle Velvel."

"Who's Uncle Velvel?" Stanley asked.

"Velvel was Grandpa and Great-Aunt Sophie's brother—back in the old country."

"Which old country?"

"Romania," his mother answered.

"Uh-oh." Stanley thought of were-wolves and vampires, and wondered if the box contained fangs, wolfsbane, or soil from the Transylvanian homeland.

Stanley's mother gave him a quick peck on the cheek. "I'll be back soon. Dad should be home in about an hour. He's leaving work early tonight." And with those words she disappeared into snowflakes swirling outside.

CHAPTER TWO

∽

The Magic Menorah

Stanley gingerly tiptoed up the stairs to the musty attic. He wondered, *What could possibly be in the box that Grandpa Abe has to have tonight, the first night of Chanukah?*

Stanley found the trunk right away, tucked under the window. He undid the latch and slowly lifted the wooden lid. As the rusted hinges creaked Stanley peeked inside. He pushed away an old army blanket, a frayed baby quilt, and a bundle of some yellowed letters tied with a rose-colored velvet ribbon. He reached deep into the trunk and pulled out a package covered with brown paper and faded stamps, and tied up with twine. Stanley shook it and heard something rattle. Was it bones? With the original soil from an old vampire coffin? Should he open it? His mother hadn't said not to. So he tugged gently at the twine, carefully untying the small knots. Stanley paused a moment and took a deep breath as he removed the brown paper and opened the box. He slowly unwrapped a soft, worn roll of cloth, making sure nothing would break or fly out, like maybe a bat. A large, dusty old menorah was in the center. Stanley eyed the tarnished brass. *A menorah,* he thought. *Why would anyone send this old thing all the way to America?*

He took a corner of the cloth and wiped the Chanukah lamp. The more he rubbed, the shinier and shinier the menorah became. Dust and caked dirt crumbled away. Stanley picked up the menorah to get a closer look. There were Hebrew letters engraved in the base and braided designs on each branch of the candelabrum all the way up to the candle-holders. Just as he finished cleaning the *shammash* to a golden gleam a thick veil of smoke arose from the menorah. Stanley felt the slats of the attic floor tremble beneath him. Out of the cloud of smoke an ancient-looking man appeared. He wore a moth-eaten black woolen overcoat and an old felt hat.

"Where did you come from? Who are y-you?" Stanley stammered, frozen with fear. Any bit of courage he had escaped like the smoke from the *hannukiah*.

"Who am *I*?" the old man said, dusting off his overcoat. "Who are *you*? And what do you want?" he continued.

"What do *I* want?" Stanley sputtered.

"Listen, *boychik,* you rubbed the *schmutz* off of that lamp, and just like a genie, *poof,* here I am." The old man sat down on the trunk and blew his nose with a raggedy gray handkerchief.

"A genie? My father's read me fairy tales about them. Genies are big and strong. Bare chested. They live in faraway places. With silk turbans and magic flying carpets."

"Genie schmeeny, I am who I am—an old man with a crumpled hat and this *schmatteh* for an overcoat. Where I come from, who could afford a turban, let alone a fancy carpet? Between you and me, to *schlep* around in this cold weather without a nice warm coat, you'd have to be a little *meshugah.*" The old man lifted his head and sniffed the air. "Do I smell cooking? You know, after all these years of being cooped up in that menorah, I could use a nice nosh."

Hoping that his mother had come back from the store, Stanley climbed down the stairs with the menorah in his hands and placed it in the window. The old man grumbled as he followed Stanley into the empty kitchen. "*Oy,* those stairs are hard on old legs. You'd think through the centuries, *poof,* I go from here to there, I'd be in better shape, but I'm not. I am tired and winded. I could use a nice glass of tea."

"Do you mean cup of tea?" Stanley asked.

The old man, out of breath, nodded.

"Glass, cup, what's the difference? But a glass would be fine. And if you should happen to have some *rugelach* or a piece of honey cake, I wouldn't complain." Stanley filled the copper kettle with water, set it on the stove, and looked for a little treat. "So," the old man sighed as he sat down, waiting for the water to boil, "should I call you Stan or Stanley?"

"Stanley," answered Stanley, surprised. "How do you know my name?"

"Don't ask. I see and hear many things in that lamp. Call me Fishel."

Stanley had never heard such a strange name. "Did you say 'Fish Meal?'"

"No, no, no," the old man said. "*Fish-el.* My name is Fishel. It means 'little fish' in Yiddish. Like a guppy. So," Fishel said again after taking a bite of the raspberry *rugelach,* "what can I do for you?"

"What do you mean?" Stanley leaned his head on his hand, looking confused.

"What do you mean, what do I mean? You summoned me from that lamp." He pointed toward Velvel's old brass menorah. "The person who releases me receives all the treasures between heaven and earth. Everyone knows, you rub a brass lamp till you're ready to *plotz,* you get three wishes."

"Three wishes?" Stanley asked.

Fishel shook his head back and forth, and looked upward. "What I get myself mixed up in. *Oy gevalt.* Three wishes. It's standard. After the third wish I return to the menorah," the old man replied, impatiently tapping his fingers on the table.

"While you're thinking, I'll have my tea and poke around a little." Fishel stood up and began to examine the pots simmering on the stove. He put his nose into one, closed his eyes, and smelled the applesauce. "Needs cinnamon," he mumbled.

Stanley rolled his eyes, thinking of his mother going out to the store for cinnamon, which had gotten him into this situation in the first place. "Yeah, I know," he said.

Fishel lifted the lid of another pot. Matzoh balls were bobbing in the chicken soup. "Ah, *kneidlach*. You mind?" he asked.

Without waiting for an answer, he dipped a ladle into the soup and scooped up a fluffy white matzoh ball. Stanley watched him slurp some noodles from the soup off a thick wooden spoon and then dip into some potato kugel, helping himself to the family's C h a n u k a h meal. "It's been a long time since I had such *hamisher* food. You'd think I hadn't eaten in years. Come to

think of it, I haven't," Fishel laughed. "Enough," he finally said, patting his full belly. "I'm satisfied. So? *Nu* already? What's it going to be?"

"Well"—Stanley paused—"what do people usually ask for?"

"What do people usually ask for?" the old man repeated. "The usual: Fame. Fortune. Happiness. You name it. I've heard it. It's up to you."

CHAPTER THREE

The First Wish

Fishel asked, "By the way, did I tell you about the riddles?"

"Riddles?" Stanley looked confused.

"For every wish I grant you, you first have to answer a riddle. Are you ready?" asked Fishel. Stanley nodded. "What walks on four legs in the morning, two legs at midday, and three legs in the evening?"

"A mouse," Stanley said, proudly.

"A *mouse?*" the old man repeated, looking confused.

"It scurries up cupboards in the

morning, begs for food on its hind legs in the afternoon, and gets its paw stuck in a mousetrap at night."

"Not bad, not bad at all, but the answer is man. He crawls when he's born, walks on two legs during his life, and hobbles with a cane in his old age."

Stanley looked at the floor, disappointed. After a moment of thinking he said, "You never told me I had to answer the riddle *correctly*. You only said answer the riddle. And I did."

Fishel squinted, lifting Stanley's chin with his finger. "Who do you think you're playing games with, sonny boy?" But then he said with a smile, "I have to admit you're right. This one's on me, but the next two riddles, no fooling around. So, what's your first wish?"

Stanley thought that if he was famous, he'd be able to do whatever he wanted with anyone he chose, and he'd probably be too busy to spend Chanukah with his family. He said out loud, "I wish for fame."

No sooner had the magical words been said than a long line of people formed in Stanley's yard. Some were banging on the front door. In no time at all they were chanting, "Stan-ley, Stan-ley, Stan-ley!" At first Stanley felt as famous as a star, but when he went outside to meet his adoring fans, they mobbed him. Everyone seemed to want something from him. A lock of his hair. A piece of his shirt. Stanley ran back inside and moaned.

"This isn't fame," he explained to Fishel. "This is nuts. Where's my name in bright lights? The autograph seekers? Other famous people?"

Fishel shrugged. "In my village, people came from far and wide to see the rabbi and seek his advice and blessings. They stood for hours, in all sorts of weather, *shvitzing* when it was hot, shivering when it was cold, just to see and hear such a humble person. Bringing a little bit of comfort and happiness to anyone who found his doorstep was more than enough for him. This was his kind of fame."

Stanley sighed loudly. "How am I supposed to do that? I don't know the answers to many questions."

Fishel elbowed him gently. "Go. I'll help you."

Stanley went back outside to meet the crowd that had gathered in his yard. Fishel stood by his side, invisible to the crowd who flocked to see Stanley. He and Stanley began to listen to question after question.

A woman in a red hat asked, "What is the meaning of life?"

Stanley scratched his head. Fishel muttered some words under his breath and Stanley repeated them: "Does anyone know the meaning of life?"

The woman smiled knowingly and walked away. Everyone nodded.

A man with a bushy mustache cried out, "Can you give my family a blessing?"

Fishel whispered, "*L'chaim.* To life."

Stanley remembered what his grandparents always said. "As long as you have your health, everything else in life will be okay." There were knowing sighs of agreement all the way to the end of the winding line upon hearing such simple, but wise, words. Stanley smiled modestly.

A child in the crowd pushed himself up to Stanley to ask, "Will my parents live forever?"

"Forever is a long time," Stanley spurted out without waiting for Fishel this time. He thought of his own parents—his mother's mouthwatering treats, her warm smile, his father's little jokes and story-telling at bedtime—so he answered, "They will live forever in your heart and mind."

You could hear an "A-a-ah" echo throughout the crowd.

Now it was Fishel's turn to smile. One by one, Stanley finished answering their questions. When everyone had left, Fishel asked impishly, "Is fame what you expected?"

"No. It's not as much fun as I thought, but still, it felt good to be able to help so many people. Like you said about the rabbi. Maybe that comes with fame."

Fishel raised his eyebrow. "One more customer," he announced.

Stanley looked down and saw a shaggy puppy at the front door gazing up at him, wagging his tail. "Are you lost? Do you need me to help you, too?" he asked the dog. Stanley picked up the puppy, who promptly rewarded him with a sloppy lick on the nose. Stanley glanced at the name tag hanging from the dog's leather collar. He couldn't believe what it said: "HI! I'M FAME. I BELONG TO STANLEY GREEN."

Stanley hugged Fame close to his chest as he looked quizzically at Fishel.

"Now you really have Fame." Fishel winked.

So Famc is what Stanley got. His first wish had come true.

CHAPTER FOUR

∽

The Second Wish

Fishel relaxed at the kitchen table and sipped the tea Stanley had made for him earlier. Stanley filled a bowl with water for Fame and wondered what was taking his mother so long at the corner store. He glanced at the clock over the stove, and the second hand remained still. Why wasn't it moving?

"One wish down, two to go," Fishel announced. "Hmm, I wonder what you'll wish for this time," he said, eyeing the platter of dreidel-shaped cookies beside him. He helped himself to one and dunked it in the tea. "But we mustn't forget the next riddle."

Stanley was disappointed that Fishel had remembered the riddles.

The old man grinned crookedly and began, "If a rooster's on the north side of a roof and lays an egg, which way will the egg fall? Think, now. Take your time."

Stanley scratched his chin. "South?"

The old man's grin widened.

"No, I meant east," said Stanley.

"You're sure?" Fishel asked.

"I think so," Stanley insisted.

"You're positive that's your answer."

"Yes," said Stanley.

"*Roosters* don't lay eggs. *Hens* do!"

"That was a trick question!" Stanley squealed. "That's not fair!"

"Who said life is fair?" Fishel chuckled.

"You promised me all the treasures between heaven and earth."

"I gave you a puppy, didn't I?" Fishel chomped on the rest of the cookie.

Stanley looked at Fame and scratched him behind the ears. "Well, yes, but—"

"But nothing. I'll give you this wish also. But this is the last time."

Stanley sighed with relief. "I wish for a fortune of gold," he said out loud, remembering the tales Grandpa Abe had told him of pirates and the stories his father had read from *The Arabian Nights*. No sooner had the magical words of the wish been uttered than latkes appeared, piled as high as Stanley's head. "*This* isn't what I wished for," Stanley said with a huff.

Fame began to eat the latkes, and the more

he ate, the more appeared. "Where is my money? My wealth? My sacks of gold?" Stanley stamped his foot on the floor.

"Stanley, Stanley, Stanley." The old man shook his head. "These are *stacks* of gold—golden fried potato pancakes!"

"This isn't fortune!" Stanley protested. "I wanted to be rich!"

Fishel cleared his throat. "In my village there was a woman who married a poor potato farmer. Every Chanukah she would search for a *shtetl* that was poorer than hers, and believe me, that wasn't so hard to find. She'd take a horse and wagon and set out with enough potato pancakes to feed that entire village for all eight nights of the holiday. She looked forward to the holiday throughout the year. There wasn't a villager who could say that she hadn't led a rich and full life."

Stanley looked down at his abundant plate, overflowing with potato pancakes, on the kitchen table. "We'll need a village, then, because I'll never be able to eat all these latkes alone," he said, shaking his head and still feeling let down.

Fishel smiled at him. "*Bubeleh,* I have got an idea. Come here, my young friend, and bring a bunch of those latkes with you. Since I don't have a fancy flying carpet, this will have to do." Fishel drew Stanley close. His woolen coat enveloped them both. Stanley couldn't see a thing.

CHAPTER FIVE

❧

Back in Time

In what seemed like an instant, the coat opened and Stanley found himself standing in front of a tiny house with a broken, weather-beaten porch. In the window facing the cobblestone street was an old, tarnished brass menorah. *It looks just like the one from the attic,* Stanley thought to himself.

Horse-drawn carts trotted by parked cars as the moon glowed and light from a lamppost flickered on the frosted, cracked windowpanes. Stanley stood outside with Fishel, Fame faithfully by his side, as he shivered in the snow and stared inside the house. He could see a large family gathered around a long wooden table. Boys and girls filled the entire small room. They peeled the few potatoes between them, all the while talking and laughing. The mother and father looked up from chopping onions and noticed Stanley watching them. They beckoned for him to come in, but he stood still, not quite knowing what to do. The father whispered something to a frail boy dressed in tattered clothes who looked to be about Stanley's age. The boy got up from his stool and came outside to greet Stanley.

Fame wagged his fluffy tail. The
boy's big toe stuck out from the
front of his worn-out shoes,
and Fame gave it a lick.

"Sorry," said Stanley, pulling
on Fame's leash, feeling embarrassed.

"Oh, that's okay, his tongue felt
warm," said the boy. "Um, my parents
thought you looked lost." The boy bent
down and patted Fame's head. He spoke
only to Stanley and Fame. He didn't seem
to see Fishel at all.

Stanley handed the boy the plate of
latkes. "Would you please take these? I
couldn't possibly eat them all by myself!
And you have so many brothers and sisters
and relatives."

"Oh, thank you. Come in," said the

boy. His eyes glistened, filled with held-back tears.

"What's wrong?" Stanley asked.

"It's from the onions my parents have been chopping for latkes!" The boy sniffed and laughed. He wiped his eyes with the corner of his shirtsleeve.

Stanley burst out laughing along with him. And then he felt a pang, remembering his mother.

The family squeezed together to make room at the table for Stanley. As they ate, Stanley glanced around. The house was dark and bare except for the glow of the Chanukah candles. The light from the wicks in the oil warmed the room even as a cold draft came through the windows. Stanley pulled up his jacket collar.

A little girl with curly red hair tugged at his sleeve. "You must be very rich to share so many latkes," she said, smiling.

"S-shush, Sophie," the boy said to her, "that's not polite." He looked at Stanley. "Little sisters," he said, and rolled his eyes.

"But, Velvel," said little Sophie, "someday we're going to be rich too."

"Our older brother, Abe, left on a boat just a week ago," explained Velvel as he turned toward Stanley. "He's going to send back money for us to come over the ocean to be with him in America. Someday the whole family will be together again!" exclaimed Velvel as he hugged his sisters and brothers and little cousins.

Stanley watched Velvel and his family and thought of his own warm, comfortable home, his kitchen filled with plenty of delicious food for the Chanukah celebration, and his parents. His eyes welled with tears. "It's the onions," he said to Velvel.

Fishel had been standing in the corner near the fireplace, the embers burning low, listening patiently. Stanley glanced over at him and nodded that it was time to go when he saw the younger children rubbing their eyes and Velvel yawning. Stanley thanked everyone and they thanked him. Velvel scratched Fame, who gave him one last lick while he and Stanley hugged good-bye. Stanley noticed that Velvel's eyes were the same color blue as his.

"So, how come you wanted to leave so

soon? You didn't even stay for the dreidel spinning," Fishel said nonchalantly as he dusted off his coat in the street.

"Maybe I miss eating latkes with my own family. Even spinning the dreidel with my little cousins!" Stanley admitted to Fishel. "I do have fortune. Back home."

"You're a real little *mensch*," said Fishel.

So fortune is what Stanley got. His second wish had come true.

CHAPTER SIX

The Third Wish

Fishel folded Stanley safely into the flaps of his coat, and in a swirl and a blink Stanley was back in the warmth of his own kitchen. He saw the streetlight stream through the large picture window overlooking his front yard. Stanley glanced at the little pots of herbs lining the windowsill and the spice jar of cinnamon next to the bubbling applesauce. He let out a deep breath. Home. Fishel heaved a great sigh, anticipating his return to the Chanukah lamp after granting Stanley his third wish. It dawned on him he could be inside the menorah a year, or one hundred years.

"Last riddle. Last wish." Fishel sighed again. "What's the difference between a *schlemiel* and a *schlimazl*?"

Stanley looked at him in silence. Stanley had heard his grandpa use those strange-sounding words about some of the family members, but he didn't understand them. "I give up," Stanley said, realizing that if he couldn't solve this riddle, he would never get his third and final wish.

"Pour me some chicken soup," Fishel ordered.

Stanley looked at him questioningly, but poured. He spilled a little bit on the sleeve of Fishel's coat. "Sorry," apologized Stanley.

"Nothing to be sorry about. You got the riddle."

"I did?" Stanley looked confused.

"A *schlemiel* is the person who *spills* the soup on the *schlimazl*. Not that I'm calling myself a *schlimazl,* mind you. So, *nu,* what's your last wish?" Fishel asked.

Stanley hesitated. He looked at his puppy. "I have Fame."

"That you do," Fishel agreed, "even though, maybe I shouldn't remind you, you're not so famous."

Stanley went from room to room and looked at the tiny gifts his parents had scattered throughout the house. "I have fortune."

"Yup, from where I sit, kiddo, you've got that, too." Fishel nodded.

"I think I already have happiness."

"You think? You're not sure?"

"Well, can I save my last wish while I am deciding?"

Fishel hesitated. "In all my years in this genie business, I have to admit no one's ever asked me that. You're the first. Not that I wouldn't mind staying awhile, but if you don't ask for the full amount, I won't be able to go back in the menorah and be there to grant three wishes to someone else someday, like maybe your child. This is a tough one. And I thought I'd heard it all. Saving a wish." Fishel shook his head back and forth and went into the living room to lie down on the couch. He propped a throw pillow behind his tired head and closed his eyes. "Ah, *boychik,* this reminds me of something years ago. . . ." He let his voice trail off, lost in his own thoughts. "I've got a sad story to tell."

"Another story?" Stanley asked.

"Another story. Sit down. Listen."

Stanley sat on the floor beside the couch, with Fame sprawled out on the rug at his feet. He gently stroked Fame, who curled up with his head on Stanley's lap.

CHAPTER SEVEN

⌘

Velvel's Story

Fishel opened his eyes, tossed a woolen afghan over his long, spindly legs, and began the story. "Years ago, across the ocean in a foreign land, there was a boy about your age named Velvel."

"Like the Velvel I met, or like my Great-Uncle Velvel?"

"One and the same," Fishel continued.

"I knew he looked familiar!" Stanley cried. "From old family pictures."

"Velvel had this very same old brass menorah. One night, *erev* Chanukah, just like this one, he left the menorah in the window like you saw it: old and tarnished. But he didn't have time to shine it. There were too many other things to do. Like try to find some potatoes to eat. Now, after you left with Fame, and all the latkes had been eaten, and the wicks in the oil had burned down to stubs in the little brass cups of the candelabrum, Velvel was about to take the corner of his old, ragged shirt and shine the dull brass."

"Did he? Did he get three wishes?" Stanley asked, excited.

Fishel sighed, this time shaking his head no. "I'm just a genie, not a miracle worker. It was the beginning of a very hard time for the world. A war. I've often thought if he could have made one wish, he could have saved himself and most of his family. But he never had the chance. Soldiers came and took them away. Little Sophie, your great-aunt, hid and managed to escape. She put the menorah in a box under a bed of straw in the attic loft, where the family used to sleep. The menorah was sent to their older brother, Abe, in America. To keep it in the family. Forever. A year later Sophie followed across the ocean."

"*My* Grandpa Abe?" Stanley asked.

Fishel nodded yes. "And that's how your Uncle Velvel's menorah found its way to your attic," Fishel said. "And I've been waiting to be summoned ever since."

"I wish I could have given my third wish to Velvel," Stanley sighed sadly.

"Ah, if only it worked like that," Fishel muttered.

"You know, my wishes of fame and fortune have taught me something. My third wish," Stanley added, "is to be with my family. My *whole* family. Here."

No sooner had the magical words been said than Stanley heard his parents in the dining room and his little cousins chasing one another around the dining-room table. Stanley hugged and kissed them. Fame jumped up and down yelping, running after them in a circle.

"I see you have already made friends with your Chanukah gift," said Stanley's father, patting Fame's little furry head.

Stanley's mother pressed her lips to Stanley's forehead. "Darling, you're not coming down with a sore throat? You had out a glass with some hot tea in it."

Stanley laughed. "I'm fine, Mom. Really. I wouldn't wish for anything more."

CHAPTER EIGHT

cVs

Eight Days of Chanukah

Stars twinkled in the sky above. Great-Aunt Sophie arrived with her arms full of gifts. She gave her mushy, wet kisses, and Uncle Max his big bear hugs. And this time Stanley gave them each a big hug back. All the cousins made a mess once again of Stanley's things. The house got hot and stuffy. But Stanley didn't mind. He said the prayers while lighting the rainbow-colored wax candle with the *shammash* in the menorah. As they ate the latkes he thought of Uncle Velvel being the same age as him so long ago.

As the Chanukah candles burned brightly in the window, Grandpa's eyes filled with tears. He pulled Stanley close and held him.

"Thank you for doing such a nice job on Velvel's menorah. It's shinier than I even remember. I haven't been able to look at it for all these years," he sighed, touching the warm, glowing brass, "until now. I'm going to be eighty this year. Velvel would have been seventy. It's been too long." He let out a long, deep breath, and Stanley felt Grandpa's heart beating against his.

Grandpa Abe kissed him on the top of his head and ruffled his hair. "This menorah is for you, Stanley. My brother Velvel would have wanted you to have it," Grandpa said. "And so do I. For your children and theirs."

Maybe Fishel was a miracle worker after all, thought Stanley. Grandpa Abe was no longer acting sad and silent on Chanukah. He wiped the sweat from his brow with a white handkerchief he pulled from the pocket of his woolen jacket, and when he smiled at Stanley, the twinkle in his eyes reminded him of Fishel. Suddenly Stanley realized that Fishel was nowhere to be seen. Had he disappeared with the third wish? Vanishing without even saying good-bye?

Eight days later, when Chanukah was over, Stanley carefully brought the old brass menorah back up to the attic. He wrapped it in the same soft, worn cloth and placed it in the box under the old army blanket and frayed baby quilt in the back of the trunk. Now he noticed that the yellowed letters tied with a ribbon were to Grandpa Abe from his family back across the ocean so very long ago.

As he closed the lid to the trunk he stared at it. Would Fishel return next year if he shined the menorah? Would he ever see Fishel again someday? Stanley knew in his heart he could ask for no more. All he needed was right here at home, safe and sound, surrounded by the love of his family. So happiness is what Stanley got. His third and final wish had finally come true.

That night Stanley thought he heard rattling in the attic. Or was it from the kitchen below? He and Fame tiptoed downstairs to find a steaming glass of tea on the kitchen table and a few stray *rugelach* crumbs on a napkin. Stanley felt a wonderful warmth inside. And he realized that there are some things in life that are better left unexplained.

"Good-bye, Fishel, and thank you," Stanley said to the air. "Happy Chanukah."

Glossary

boychik (BOY-chick) *Yiddish:* a term of endearment and affection for a boy

bubeleh (BUB-eh-lah) *Yiddish:* a term of endearment meaning "darling," "dear child," or "little doll"

challah (CHA-la; with the gutteral *ch* of the Scottish *loch*)) *Hebrew:* an egg-enriched bread served at a Shabbat meal

Chanukah or **Hanukkah** (HAH-noo-ka) *Hebrew:* an eight-day Festival of Lights celebrating the victory of the Maccabee warriors over Antiochus, the Syrian/Greek ruler who destroyed the Jewish Temple and tried to force the Jews to worship many gods instead of one

erev (EH-riv) *Hebrew:* the night before

feh (feh!) *Yiddish:* an exclamation showing distaste

Fishel (FISH-el) *Yiddish:* a boy or man's name that means "little fish"

hamisher (HAY-mish-er; rhymes with *Danish*) *Yiddish:* homey, cozy, warm

hannukiah (HAH-noo-KEY-a) *Hebrew:* the Chanukah candelabrum

kneidlach (k-NAYD-loch; the gutteral *ch* sound in Hebrew and Yiddish is like the Scottish *loch,* or in music, *Bach*) *Yiddish:* a matzoh-meal dumpling usually the size of a ping-pong ball, served in chicken soup

kugel (KOO-gull) *Yiddish:* a noodle or potato pudding

latke (LOT-kah) *Yiddish:* a potato pancake fried in oil and eaten during Chanukah

L'chaim (Le CHIGH-em) *Hebrew:* a celebratory toast over raised glasses of wine; meaning "To life."

matzoh (MOTT-sa) *Yiddish and Hebrew:* unleavened flat bread that has not risen. (no yeast).

menorah (min-NO-rah) a nine-armed candelabrum; eight arms representing each night of Chanukah. The ninth is the shammash that lights the other candles

mensch (MENCH; rhymes with *bench*) *Yiddish;* a good, decent, honorable person

meshugah (mi-SHU-geh); *Yiddish:* crazy; a nutty person

mitzvah (MITS-vah) *Hebrew:* a good deed or a kind act

nosh (NOSH) *Yiddish:* a litle snack

Nu? (NEW) *Yiddish:* Well? So? (Always in the form of a question)

Oy gevalt! (OY-ge-VAHLT) *Yiddish:* an exclamation or cry of astonishment and amazement

plotz (PLOTZ) *Yiddish:* to burst, explode

rabbi (RA-bye) *Hebrew:* the religious leader of a Jewish congreation and synagogue; ordained spiritual teacher

rugelach (RUG-ah-loch) *Yiddish:* a small, crescent-rolled pastry filled with raisins, ground nuts, cinnamon, sugar, and raspberry jam

schlemiel (shleh-MEAL) *Yiddish:* an inept fool; a klutzy, clumsy person; simpleton

schlep (SHLEP) *Yiddish:* to carry

schlimazl (schli-MAHZ-el) an unlucky person; a ne'er-do-well; a loser

schmatteh (SHMAH-tah) *Yiddish:* a rag

schmutz (SHMUTZ) *Yiddish:* dirt

shammash (SHAH-mas) *Hebrew:* It is also referred to as the helper candle because it is used to light the other eight candles on the menorah. The *shammash* is usually set apart from the other candles.

shtetl (SHTET-el) *Yiddish:* a little town or small village, particularly in Jewish eastern European communities before World War II

schvitzing (SHVITS-ing) *Yiddish:* sweating or perspiring a lot

Torah (TOE-rah) *Hebrew:* the first five books of the Bible